Two
REMARKABLE
NOVELETTES
Volume 1

Sheron Mingo Y

First Paperback, Fictional Edition, December 2024
ISBN: 979-8-9855724-3-8 (Paperback)
ISBN: 979-8-9855724-5-2 (Hardcover)

SuperMementosYea LLC

Dedication

To my dear mother, Megan, who with God gave me life and champions life, with resilience: now with declined health competencies and a childlike (sweet and rascal) demeanor. So much she has generously given. Yet, much has been filched from her. She was eager for my literary debut but can no longer comprehend that I have written literary books nor read and celebrate my books.

Dedication also to every child or person with a passion and a dream to succeed. Perfect your craft and realize your dreams even as life happens; even when barriers near and far distract and impede your efforts.

Acknowledgment

Thanks to God Almighty, my truest love and unconditional friend, in heaven and on earth. God sustains and endows me with ingenuity and timeless talent to write, create and transform readers via multiple genres. Without God, I would not be. And to my editor and cover designer.

My writing is influenced by Charles Dickins, Edgar Allan Poe, Rebecca West, Brad Leithauser and many others. I revere their genius abilities to create intriguing plots, settings, characters and dialogue. Each of my literary influencers infuse humor commingled with the stark realities of life throughout their stories that compel readers to laugh, cogitate, and relate: if not change.

Introduction

Revel in endless laughter as you read, "TWO REMARKABLE NOVELETTES: VOLUME 1". The novelettes in this volume fuse US and Guyanese cultures with reality and embellishments to deliver indelible literary fiction.

"Communion with Maud" set in the US, and "Turn Around Age" set in Guyana, expertly unwrap this first volume. Both novelettes are cleverly written with artistic flare and cultural verve—to present the wretched and enchanting facets of life based on encounters, observation, scrutiny and cultural deconstructs. Stories are timeless and free of profanity to delight diverse readers.

Expect colloquial dialogues, expressions and nuances with captivating South American and US settings, and cuisines that authenticate and distinguish characters' cultural identities and geographical settings. Readers will enjoy vivid, humorous characters with relatable societal dilemmas: ideal for quick, gratifying literary reads.

Enjoy this paperback version and those upcoming in Volumes 2, 3 and 4 and consider each novelette the witty and literary melding of the hearts of diverse cultures. Each Volume will deliver two new Novelettes, and each are shorter than novellas yet longer than short stories. All invite young and mature readers to embrace and discuss life and humor through literature in schools, libraries, social gatherings and around dinner tables.

Please leave a 5* review on any intriguing aspect of this book.

Contents

1
Communion
With
Maud
8,020 WORDS

Communion With Maud

Columbus Day floated in and out with a week of sales and festive discoveries. Now Saturday comes unstirred. Millie smiles, although her husband is six-plus hours and oceans away on an international business trip. She will rove today and enjoy holy serenity with God. Sweet, sacred Sabbath calm, is all she needs to encounter and enjoy.

Millie grooms herself slowly, with grace. Then she slips her loveliness into a wool suit. She grabs her vintage Liz Claiborne handbag and hurries out the door at 10:25 am. A moderate October breeze steers her down Beach Channel Drive, towards the Gaston subway, in Queens, New York. She frowns at pigeon feces as she climbs dusty stairs and swipes her metro card. A green light lets her through and she boards the "A" train and takes a window seat. Her sixty-five minutes commute should get her to Balm SDA Church for the last half of Sabbath Service. *I'll mend my tardy ways, and be punctual, next time*, she thinks.

Today marks the first Saturday that Millie's husband is away internationally since their three years of courtship and marriage. He chose the Columbus holiday week for his business and travel expedition. But he will return in twenty-four hours.

Millie sits erect in her seat, as the train rushes, and rubs a thumb over her pearly manicure. She loves its flawless feel—her manicurist is a definite genius. Her handbag drops to the floor as the train veers and fills the air with clanks and screeches. She snatches her handbag off of the dingy train floor and stares beyond the graffiti-smeared window to the pureness of the sunshine and the evergreen trees swaying in the breeze.

Calmness, larger than any train's ruckus, envelops her. She anticipates a pleasant time worshiping God at Balm.

The train glides across the Rockaway Bay, inching Millie closer to Balm. Her stomach trembles since she can't swim and may not be lucky enough to float should the train derail. Her anxious stares search the gray water dreading a kiss from its ominous lips. Silver-bellied fish flick conspicuously and create gigantic furrows across the water's surface.

Millie shudders and ponders what snakes and menacing creatures the countless species of fish evade as everything often evades something.

A lovely cinnamon-colored, goddess-like woman, with cellphone in hand, boards the train at Broad Channel and sits next to Millie. They exchange brief smiles.

"Love you," the woman types into her cellphone.

Millie squints her eyes to pry discreetly from the

woman's cellphone.

"Love you More," the person in the woman's phone texts back. The woman's lean face flashes a serene smile.

"I love you the most," The woman texts back. A smile lingers on her face. She looks angelic with hazel eyes and a pair of comely dimples on her youthful cheeks. Perhaps a newlywed because of her bliss. Sleeked, auburn hair parted down the middle rests on her shoulders. She is fashionable in beige designer garbs and wears a humongous diamond ring and a silver wedding band. Her voice is perky, but pleasant as she whispers what she writes in her text.

Millie wonders if this woman's loved one is far away or will join her at home. She savors her peeps of the text exchanges as if she views a movie scene, but without popcorn and soda. She is as happy with her Georgie as this ebullient woman seems with her sweet love, and there's a feeling of euphoric calm and enchantment.

Millie smiles for the unflawed day and the intrigue of this cinnamon-being sitting beside her.

There's a sudden loud, but familiar screech of train brakes, and Millie and other commuters groan. Their train, crossing the bridge, comes to an abrupt halt and may be delayed for minutes. Worst is the reality that the train sits ominously over the bay, between Broad Channel and Howard Beach stations, albeit closer to Howard Beach. Millie dreads sitting over expansive water that could result in her demise should the bridge collapse. The cinnamon woman suspends texting and looks at Millie, with the unuttered question of, *why now?*

An elderly Asian man, who sits two seats away from Millie, says, "Not again. This happened yesterday." He is dressed in khaki uniform and seems to do maintenance work.

"That's why I dodge the fare," A robust Hispanic woman, who wolfs a bag of Doritos chips and looks 30+ says. "This transit system gone bonkers, Y nadie lo arregla."

Millie ponders whether the flawed NYC transit system is duping commuters or shorted by unscrupulous straphangers who evade fares and hence the present disrepair. She peeps at the woman then at the man, discreetly, to not add to his annoyance. What could she do but pay her obligated share of transit fares and not litter subways and trains. She studies the lovely coach watch on her wrist.

"I don't need scary delays today," Millie thinks. "I just need to get to Balm for some blessings." She glances at the other commuters. Ten percent are professionally dressed for work or formal commitments. Others seem to be tourists returning to Brooklyn or Manhattan from their October-sunup-Rockaway beach surfs or swims before the colder fall weather arrives and therefore, they show little worries or hurry.

The PA system crackles, for seconds, and is finally audible. Everyone hushes for an update.

"Please remain seated while we check the problem, ladies and gentlemen. We will resume service momentarily," the train announcer says. "We apologize for this delay. Thanks for your patience."

The Asian man dressed in kaki, scowls and sucks his teeth. Then he beats the window with his fists. Millie and others instinctively empathize with him since travelers need to be on their way. Two train operators walk to the middle of the car and open one of its doors with an alien-looking key.

"What's wrong. What's wrong?" People ask shouting over each other.

"We're not sure," the operator says. They descend rails on the side of the train to assess the problem.

Some passengers capture the scene with cameras and cellphones to serve thriller stories to news outlets, or tourists to their families and social platforms. Millie's hands tremble from the discomfort of being trapped over the bay for minutes. Hence, she whispers a voiceless prayer.

"God, I'm sorry for my wrongs. Don't let this be the end of me. Restart this train and send me on my way to give my time to you on this holy Sabbath Day." Other commuters strategize, with haste, then stand and hurry towards the rear car closest to land and the Howard Beach Station.

Millie abruptly ends her prayers, grabs her purse, and follows the crowd hoping the train's anterior won't tilt with the frantic surge of passengers. Luckily, most of the train carriages are half-empty. When the hordes of passengers enter the last three cars, the train suddenly jolts into motion and resumes its journey. Everyone whistles and applauds.

"Please take your seats, ladies and gentlemen," the train conductor says. "We had breaks malfunction but service has resumed."

My life in the Rockaways, Millie thinks and releases a huge sigh. *The boardwalk is lovely, and it's nice to hear birds sing outside my windows and see the sunrise, but crossing the bay is a constant bother.* Nonetheless, she looks forward to her time at Balm and the blessings she will receive.

Millie smiles when the cinnamon-goddess like woman slips her a Jehovah's Witness track, and disembarks from the train at Howard Beach, and leaves behind a flow of floral perfume.

The train arrives in Brooklyn and deposits Millie at Liberty and Atlantic Avenues. She hurries out of the dim, musty subway.

"A dollar for the old man. Give a little dollar," a raggedy man with silver dreads shuffles by and begs.

Millie presses .50¢ into his palm, and feels benevolent, like the 1% elite that performs a miniscule good. She then looks at the crystal blue sky and likes the calmness of the day. *Today is a winsome day* she thinks, *despite the earlier scare and delay with the train.*

She has visited other churches in Brooklyn. Beulah and Bethel are conservative ones with droughts of fun surprises. Members sit poised and don't clap their hands.

Most Adventists are allergic to charismatic worship. There's no bawls in tongues or stamps of holy-ghost feet. Nonetheless, Millie relishes the intrigue of visiting different Adventist churches to enjoy versions of pious worshipers' reserved amens or the claps and sways of animated members. She occasionally meets friends she hasn't seen in years. They consume impromptu lunches at their homes or hers, for Sabbath is a revered convocation enjoyed by family and friends with delicious curried chicken, soups, okra dumplings, Jamaican jerk chicken, stewed cabbages, and chats about who had fornicated with whom.

Balm SDA Church is rich with vintage eminence, having the semblance of an old Greek cathedral. Its exterior exhibits red terracotta bricks. Replicas of bible luminaries protrude from these bricks and show prophets clutching staffs and writing on scrolls.

Millie envisions camels tramping by like in B.C. and A.D. before and after Christ traversed the earth. This seemingly massive structure takes her to Bethlehem Judah, and she smiles, thinking of Christ when he fed the multitude with five barley loaves and two tiny fish. Her mouth salivates as she stands enthralled outside of Balm. Millie swallows her saliva and imagines an enticing, crispy fish sandwich. She consequently feels a thud and drops her handbag as she bumps into a lanky white boy on Liberty Avenue. Although it's wholly her fault, the boy tries to avoid a collision with Millie and almost falls.

"Sorry," she says embarrassed and steadies the disgruntled boy.

"Look where ya going, Lady." The boy says. He picks up Millie's handbag and hands it to her.

"Thanks, kid," Millie says, pleased with the civility of Brooklyn, New York. The boy turns pale grey eyes on her momentarily then grips his yellow sweater and baggy gray jeans and hurries away. Millie hugs her purse and laughs uncontrollably at the events thus far of her day and how grossly late and embarrassed she is to enter Balm. Parishioners will judge her and not the tardy train. The stalled train had delayed her an extra thirty minutes. Service usually begins at 9:15 am and ends by 1:00 pm in most SDA churches worldwide.

Nonetheless, Millie approaches the church's door with a surveyor's stroll as its clock gives twelve solemn clangs to announce noon. She has missed chunks of today's service but perhaps an hour with God will suffice. *My misdemeanors weren't too extreme,* she thinks. She was gloomy that her husband would leave for a sudden trip to his Guyana and had told him she was sick with her monthly. She did not engage in his romantic frolics and was not to be blamed. But that was six days ago, before his trip; she will make recompense in twenty-four hours when he returns.

Millie enters Balm's restroom in the foyer. The soles of her shoes pat gray marble tiles as a pleasant lavender scent engages her nose. She inhales prodigiously and enjoys the freshness even as she powders her face and scrutinizes her teeth. She welcomes every drip of luxury life gives; although, she's neither rich nor poor. The empty restroom witnesses her vanity, as she enjoys the Sabbath respite from her week of bustle. She pats her suit and hurries into the sanctuary with unsuppressed curiosity and thrusts her frame ahead of the usher.

Her eyes love the church's eggshell walls with gold accents, but she's disappointed with its meager interior that lacks the splendid ornamentation its exterior promised and is expected in a landmark place of worship. She sinks into a blue, cushioned pew. An oblique view of the pulpit area reveals a pearly linen, tablecloth, lain over a table pregnant with trays of grape juice and unleavened bread.

Today is Holy Communion at Balm. This happens quarterly in SDA churches. Parishioners usually hear an abridged sermon, bathe each other's feet in basins of water, and eat a teensy piece of unleavened bread (symbolic of the body of Christ), with a swallow of grape juice. The deacons serve this between 12:00 and 1:00 pm, when everyone's stomach is ravenous, and mouths salivate in vain. Parishioners often stretch indecisive hands towards serving plates, unsure of which unleavened morsel is the chunkiest to grab.

Millie's stomach growls at the tease of bread and juice and she therefore reminisces of how her mother, who was a deaconess, brought home leftover communion bread and how crunchy and intriguing it was as a teen to eat the "holy" bread." Hence, she licks her lips and conjures up enticing visions of her spinach pasta at home and hopes her oven keeps it nice and warm although she will reheat it.

Balm's congregation, seated in worship, radiates diversity with blacks, Indians, whites, and Hispanic parishioners: and perhaps more. A black organist stirs keys and music flows as a burly, Asian gentleman sings, "People Need the Lord". His soulful tenor voice delivers tranquility.

Millie ignores the abrasive crooning and clapping of the senior woman in the pew behind to focus on the gentleman's rendition. But her lips twitch uncontrollably with disgust at the pesky senior woman.

Hence, Millie closes her eyes and becomes engrossed in the service, thinking of the angelic choir she will be part of if she quits her mortal gossips and overindulgences of cheesecakes and makes it to heaven—where she will be blessed with a melodious voice and a perfect figure. Then, no one will laugh at her singing and deride her croaky voice.

At 12:07 pm, a handsome pastor stands immaculately clad in a gray suit before the pulpit. "I've been accused of long-windedness," he says. He clutches the pulpit, and a chuckle emerges from his slim throat. His stylish, black Louboutin shoes glitter. This elegant pastor looks 6'2" and physically fit and can't be older than thirty-nine. He wears a broad wedding band on his manicured finger.

The band surprises Millie since SDA pastors don't usually wear wedding bands that are considered carnal and unnecessary. Perhaps nobody at Balm throws stones—not even the senior woman.

"We have no time for chitchats and loitering today," the Pastor says. "Please be mindful of the solemnity of today's sacred service. I will be brief and speak on the Passover Supper for five minutes, after which, we will wash feet, VEEEE-RY expeditiously, and partake of the sacred bread and juice," he states.

The senior woman claps, and says, "Amen. Amen for brevity." Millie blushes convinced that the pastor heard her. Offering plates float around and tithes and gifts are collected. Even kids flash dollars and coins they place pridefully in the extended offering plates. America's imposed taxes have shrunk Millie's paychecks, but God requires her 10% and gifts, hence, she tithes $309 monthly at her church. She digs into her purse, flipping between a twenty and two fifty-dollar bills, but finds no five or a single dollar bill. She had forgotten to bring her change purse.

The disappointed deacon stations his plate before her and flashes a grim smile; Millie sighs and grudgingly surrenders her twenty.

The pastor shakes his head for several seconds and says, "Jesus embodies humility. He washed his disciples' grungy feet. We must humble ourselves like Jesus! NO ONE should shirk Holy Communion. Feet washing and the emblematic bread and juice will renew our bodies and elevate our spirits. We are adulterers brothering! We sin when we lust after another man's wife or another woman's husband. We commit adultery when we worship our jobs and possessions and forsake God. Jesus' blood can cleanse us! He will FORGIVE us as He forgave the adulterous woman at the well...."

"HALLELUJAH," the congregation replies. "Jesus FORGIVES sins!"

"He forgave me for stealing Mugging's wife." A black man says, with tears in his eyes. "I'm a sorry wretch. But Jesus loves me. I'm a better me now." The attractive

Philippine woman sitting beside him hangs her head with closed eyes as if too ashamed to be seen.

Millie closes her eyes hoping that Jesus would

understand that she had had communion four Sabbaths ago at her church and wouldn't participate again before the new quarter in two months.

"Grabgo must wash them depraved feet of hers and leave Estelle's husband alone," The senior lady says. "God will surely, surely punish her and that deacon for fornicating—no adulterating. Yes. Yes. God will. Cause he's alive and watching with HIS HOLY eyeballs even if nobody thinks so."

"Whaaaa-aat? Yuh can't keep quiet for a minute?" a haggard, drowsy voice asks. Millie peeps over her left shoulder and sees a furrowed man sitting beside the senior woman. His wrinkly wrist hangs out of his grey jacket sleeves. The senior woman is dressed in black and white as a deaconess.

"You betta stay awake," the senior woman says to the man and sighs exasperatedly. Stop your sleeping and listen. That Grabgo adulterating with Estelle's husband. I hope she listening to pastor. I never, never like her prancing 'bout in them teeny, teeny dresses, and she's a deaconess. What a shame, and this church is wrong! Wrong to allow her."

"Mind yuh business," the old man says. "Yuh always in everybody's business but yuh own." His voice sounds huskier because of a crackling phlegm inside his throat. Millie is startled and jumps when the old woman slaps the back of Millie's pew with her bible, as if Millie is Grabgo, or she knows of her decision to boycott foot washing, and the juice and holy bread, and is chastising her lack of deference and humility for the service.

Millie recognizes the familiar accent and knows this boisterous couple is from her husband's Guyana, but from the countryside because their rustic, tangled lingo floods her ears. The unsettling image of a naked Grabgo and deacon prances around her mind for a future racy gossip. But now, she frowns and makes a mental note to staple the senior woman's lips if chance permits. She wonders whether she and her husband will act like these two, once age corners them. She hopes they remain gracious and mind their own business; although, occasional gossip does flavor life and whisks the mundane flow of things.

After the congregation sings "At The Cross," and the men and women quickly separate through opposite doors for feet washing, a woman with a semblance of grace enters the sanctuary. "Is anyone sitting there?" She asks the handsome Irish man with toned built and red curly hair sitting at the end of Millie's pew. She points a bejeweled index finger at the empty space between the man, and Millie who admires her ruby ring (real or fake). Her fingers gleam with crimson nail polish.

The man turns salmon red as he smiles politely and shakes his head to indicate no. He is a newly baptized member at Balm and radiates grace and piety in his charming face. He seems relaxed amid diversity and welcomes this woman and shifts in his seat to make room.

"Thank you. I'm Maud," she says and sits. She extends her shapely, brown arm.

He shakes her hand with his pearly hand and says, "I'm Luke." Both flash fetching smiles.

Millie's eyes skim the woman's face whose lipstick does not bleed. The satin spread of her foundation remains flawless on her ebony skin. Her hair flows in long silky braids enhancing the delightful glow on her face. Millie remembers the cinnamon goddess she had encountered on the train earlier and doesn't mind sitting beside this visitor. Her flawless face evokes images of a genius artist who never smudges defining lines. But she seems a snub for not shaking Millie's hand that is as visible as Luke's.

Some women grudge even in churches instead of caring and encouraging, Millie thinks. *We should sister-up and stop undermining each other.*

At 12:25, after feet had been expeditiously washed, the pastor and his platform participants reenter the sanctuary and service resumes.

Maud sits erect in her seat and combs her skirt with fidgety fingers. She mutters to herself and smiles all the while and seems content with life and her seat among parishioners. But Millie suddenly pinches her nose as two displeasing things become apparent. Maud smells like fermented pee and engages in constant discourse with herself. Millie slouches in denial. Her nose twitches as she peers at Maud whose stench creeps toward the surrounding pews like an insidious hailstorm.

Millie sees disconcerted parishioners rub their noses in disgust, rise from their pews and rush to the furthest parts of the church sending Maud incredulous looks. Some opt to stand with aggrieved faces and backs against the wall for the remainder of the service as if church is a heresy and the pastor spreads fallacies.

Although Maud does not seem physically wounded, Millie wonders if their actions are sinful and whether someone will soon yell "leper" to ostracize Maud and starkly contrast the good Samaritan in the bible who helped the wounded, homeless man. But Maud's gaze cages Millie whose left shoulder brushes the wall. She'd have to pass Maud to escape so she sits shackled to sighs and giggles, afraid of appearing snobbish and inciting an unholy brawl.

Maud's initial poise had muffled her reek. She suddenly changed from an African goddess to a smelly, eccentric bother.

Do first impressions resonate more than the second or the last: since someone must attract attention with a first impression and then engage and sustain that attention, Millie tilts her head and ponders. She decides that life is a chronic surprise with societal aches and oddities like Maud or pretentious colleagues whose evils remain obscure until competing for promotions and their duplicity eventually leaks through their facades. Millie toils with relationships because her winning nature often gets misinterpreted and misused. She values and agrees that friendship and connections are needed but demand commitment and tons of stress.

But is there ever a stressless relationship? Yes. Her Archie keeps their lives stressless. But who keeps people like Maud stressless? Hence, Millie embroiled in turmoil over Maud's plight pulls from memory the only poem she ever wrote, years ago, in high school that had startled her then beyond her 16 years but now made sense.

> Some societal "haves"
> Swing purses that cheat, with conceit
> To blur brazen greed,
> That flout and suppress those who should thrive.
> Most "don't haves,"
> Fling impeded hands and feet;
> Bruised with unjust defeats,
> And crave their earthly keeps
> To strive and survive,
> Without conniving traits of deceit;
> To grapple and meet dire needs.

Millie sighs heavily and looks at the preacher although she knows that preachers are humans who don't have all the answers. They share and interpret scripture, but some need empathy and rescue for themselves. At least preachers give temporary relief.—Hence, she listens to this handsome preacher.

Maud flashes a graceful smile that slides over Millie, and strips her of discomfort and intolerance. Millie frowns then shoots an obligatory grin back at Maud, hoping not to collapse from suffocation. Maud is the epitome of glee. She digs into her Duane Reade shopping bag, tossing dingy perturbing stuff at Millie's feet.

Millie flinches, and dreads what evils might grab her each time Maud shoves her hands into her dingy bag. She bemoans being flanked by this eccentric, and the wall and is unable to focus on the service. Why could Maud not be like the lovely, cinnamon sister she had encountered earlier on her trip to Balm? Perhaps Maud served a purpose in juxtaposition with that train goddess—the haves and haves-not of the 20th century. Maybe God is present in both sisters to reveal obscurities and the blatant realities of life.

From her bag, Maud extracts a soggy peanut butter sandwich encrusted with fungus. She looks at it ecstatically then begins to wolf it down; but her conscience reprimands her. Hence, she rips the sandwich in half, excavates a grimy napkin from her bag, and hands the piece of blight to Millie.

"Have piece," she says. "It'll nourish them dainty bones of yours. Found this someplace yesterday."

Millie's saliva bitters in her mouth and her stomach retches. Slime swells within her throat as she rolls her stare down Maud's ample frame. She gulps the vomit in her throat, and prays for the service to climax. Why hadn't she attended church with her aunt?

Watching her aunt's sixty-five-year-old boyfriend harvest his pimples now seems trivial compared to this woman's fumes and eccentricities. She feels lonely and wishes her husband would reconvert and ditch atheism and accompany her to weekly Saturday services because he is nicer than many of the Christians she knows.

Georgie was once an SDA Christian but did not like the cultural battles and hypocrisies of his local church. He first skipped months of service then vamoosed altogether from attending church two years ago.

Maud makes Millie empathize with the needy and Balm forces her into contrition for societal wrongs she hasn't done. Was God conscious of her dilemma? Well, this is 2007 and President G. Bush should help Maud. "Most "don't haves Fling impeded hands and feet, bruised with unjust defeats," she thinks and glances at Luke. He stands motionless with a blank smile and an alert expression. But his green eyes are cemented shut with prayer. She wonders what he supplicates and envies the peace he knows.

Millie eyeballs the Christian flag and the American flag facing each other from right and left poles on the rostrum, perhaps hurling denunciations. It seems none can separate church and state since church meddles in state matters and vis versa. All the SDA churches she knows bear these flags. She stabs the blue carpet with a perplexed stare but fails to extract a realistic answer that would erase the guilt from America or herself—perhaps God too since he doesn't seem to intervene and Maud and the desolate suffer perpetually.

Perhaps Maud is immune to neglect and comforts, but everyone needs love, and Millie can't fathom God's apparent abandonment. Perhaps this crazy woman is stronger than she could ever be. She wonders how she'd fare if her husband, Georgie, abandoned her? She couldn't survive without his love.

What would happen if she lost her job, and her family, and friends spurned her, and she becomes homeless and meaningless? She glances at her watch. The shorthand sits on twelve and the long hand points at thirty. It should be half an hour more till service ends. Maud sighs, looks reproachfully at Millie then shoves her mildewed feast into Millie's hand. "I need to focus, take this.—Okay," she says. She then enjoys the final bite of her half of sandwich.

Millie rolls her hands into inflexible fists rejecting Maud's food. The moldy glop lands on the ground. Maud stamps her feet and glares at Millie who flicks her gaze towards the ceiling to hide the guilty smirk that fills her face. She is thankful that this woman's ire is mere frustration devoid of violence.

"What, you too prissy to share my food when people starving all over?" Maud asks and snatches the piece of fungus off the carpet and shoves it at Millie. *This deranged woman is more hospitable than me*, Millie thinks. *She shares the little she has. Fearlessness and audacity must be her riches. Is she ever afraid of anyone, anything—or is she too crazy to recognize fear? Where does she shower, if ever?*

Millie thinks of her comfy baths and warm showers shared with Georgie and her heart jabs her into capitulation. "I'll eat it after service," she says, and forces the wretched thing into her vintage Liz Claiborne bag: hoping that the beige lining won't stain.

"Good," Maud replies. She chews the remnants in her mouth then rubs her feet cheerfully against the carpet and regards Millie amiably for a few seconds. Millie sighs sadly. Her acceptance of Maud's food seals their friendship. She can't help but compare Maud to the cinnamon goddess she had encountered on the train. How unalike they were. Both confident and beautiful—yet one so destitute and unhinged.

"Your ring's pretty," Maud says eying Millie's left hand. "Where's he?"

"Who?"

"The husband."

"In Guyana. A business trip."

"Ah! Cunning one." Maud leans closer, and whispers as if she shares a secret. "Cunning birds fly away to end a season." Maud's spit sprays Millie's face. Millie's hand jerks but doesn't wipe her face. She's relieved that Maud's mouth isn't rancid. She knows people whose mouths are edifices of tartar and neglect.

Millie thinks of her husband, hours and oceans away. He had taken Delta and rose high into the heavens like a dove. She trusts him but feels slightly nervous for the first time; she is unfamiliar with his exotic Guyana and its calypso, virgin jungles and the lofty Kaieteur Falls. She is ignorant of who embraces him there. This uncertainty makes her shudder.

"Call him. You hear what I say. Don't trust men. Guyanese girls snatch overseas men to get visas. They trap men with babies. I should know. It's how I'm here, and that preacher is my ex-husband before he got fancy and mighty. I come here every Saturday to remind him. Nobody in this church believes because I'm mad.—My baby dead too," Maud adds with visible tears in her eyes that melts Millie's heart since she hopes to have a living baby one day. But she thinks that Maud is crazy for claiming the pastor as her ex-husband.

I'll call Georgie after church, Millie thinks. She isn't distrusting, she decides; she's just being cautious. They were supposed to speak today anyway. This crazy woman insinuates that her Georgie is a two-timer when he is a worthy man and never could be doubted. She should ring

Maud's ears even if Maud's combat skills and physical dominance outshine hers and flouts her saneness. Perhaps parishioners will join and wrestle this woman to the ground. Not many unfortunately value a lunatic. But how could Maud implicate a devout man like the pastor as being her ex-husband?

"Call him when you get home. Men are devils. I know what I know. It's true and nothing but the truth. You hear me? You hear me?" Maud reiterates with emphatic stares.

Millie scowls and dismisses the dreadful possibility of her guileless husband as a cheat who frolics behind her back with repulsive, brazen women. Millie sulks beside the riotous Guyanese lunatic she has inherited. She has never met a nutty Guyanese before. They usually work lengthy hours and attain cars, homes and impressive bank accounts. Many educate and obtain degrees like her Georgie. She blinks pensive eyes and looks at her fashionable watch. It shows 12:33 pm.

Maud thumps the bench. Millie jumps involuntarily and is angry with herself as Maud sees and laughs. There's no escaping Maud since the wall to her left blocks potential flight. But Maud the lunatic isn't hostile and she'll survive till service ends.

"Listen to the sermon," Maud says. She throws pious stares upon the pastor, but keeps tunneling her hands into her bag and stirring up fetid smells.

It perturbs Millie that Maud could eat rancid food so cheerfully *to strive and survive without conniving traits of deceit; to grapple and meet dire needs.* Why doesn't Washington rescue America's loonies? Isn't America saving the world? Millie had helped Georgie shop and pack food and clothes for his relatives in Guyana. Now she sits in her beloved America, in 2007—where dreams are supposed to come true, next to a destitute Guyanese nut.

I don't know this woman. Am I supposed to feel guilty, Millie thinks. *But nothing is ever anybody's fault. That's the problem with our world and nobody takes the blame and fixes wrongs. This helpless woman needs love and attention and here I am judging.*

Empathy shackles Millie and she cannot spurn Maud whose ebony skin and hers radiate an African pigment that seals their heritage from the entrails of the motherland. The word "SISTER" instantly occupies her mind. *I should invite her to my home for a bath and a healthy meal.* Millie thinks but knows full well she lacks courage to do such a good but daring deed for fear of her safety and the mess Maud may create in her dainty home.

Millie is a real-estate sales assistant. She and Georgie own a comfortable home in Arverne, NY. Georgie is a realtor with a $95,000 gross income plus commissions—so they are stable and set to explore business opportunities, expand their family and manage life's bestowals.

Maud shifts her attention to Luke; although, she eyes Millie warily, as if forbidding her to move. She whispers, "Love your eyes. Where you live? I'm single. You married? Any kids?" Loudly into his ears. The bewildered man, not wishing to disrupt the service, spews answers and they commune in this manner for seconds.

Millie cannot suppress her giggles since Maud and Luke look like lovers and bliss wraps itself around Maud's face as she exploits the thrill of the moment.

Millie's work week at the real estate office (besides the Columbus Day holiday) had been dull. No clients had complained; hence, she had reorganized her two filing cabinets and counted the remaining business days of Georgie's trip. She dodged cooking and ordered in her meals or picked them up on her way home and binge watched *Girlfriends*, *Waiting to Exhale*, *Sister, Sister* and more. The week eventually dwindled away. Now she sits conscious of her encounter with Maud, the barmy intrigue.

A placid smile sits upon Maud's face. Luke, unlike her, wears an exasperated scowl all the while until Maud returns her attention to Millie who snatches her gaze off of Maud and Luke with the agility of a squirrel and sits tracing the veins in her right palm.

"Handsome men are serpents," Maud leans close and says. "Had my share of them. And that one," she points a caustic finger at Luke, "is conceited—probably a womanizer." She sighs and rolls her eyes.

Millie's side aches with suppressed laughter and she wonders how Luke's whispers could rile Maud even as Maud pitches a rancorous stare at Luke. Seems as if all the striking men in this church are accosted by Maud.

Millie agrees with Maud nonetheless because she had dated two conceitedly handsome men before she married Georgie. One was her high school boyfriend who filched her money, and in her apartment, sampled her best friend. The other was her best friend's brother, the ardent liar and underachiever, who slept instead of conducting research to write gradable college papers. He eventually ditched her, and college, to romance a married woman.

Her doting Georgie has enormous feet and flatulates when he sleeps. But he's 6'2", the height she likes for her man and has a kind voice and a virtuous heart. And she doesn't mind the flab around his stomach nor his receding hairline—just means he's happy. He'd be home in twenty-four hours. She will welcome him with eager arms and his favorite dish of barbecued fried trout and roasted carrots. She wishes he was sitting beside her with his cheerful laughter.

A plump black, and a stout white deaconess gingerly remove the tablecloth from the communion table and fold the embroidered linen fabric with bowed heads. Service would probably climax in twenty-three minutes. The pastor and his six elders wash hands in crystal bowls that sit at opposite sides of the table. They break unleavened bread into fragments and six deacons enter the isles with filled plates and serve parishioners.

Maud beams then grasps a serving plate with her left hand and a handful of the bread fragments with her right hand that she packs into her mouth. She chews vigorously and coughs open mouthed, ungraciously splattering bits; then she wipes her mouth. Her other hand finally releases the serving plate, and the agitated deacon moves on to serve other worshippers.

Millie disapproves of Maud's behavior and peeks at Maud through the corners of her eyes not wishing to make eye contact and don a bogus smile. She may be mistaken, but is somehow convinced that this eccentric woman knows how and when to behave in a church.

Maud indignantly twists her mouth into a vigorous scowl that exposes even white teeth. *She really is an attractive woman,* Millie thinks. *Better looking than many of the ardent snobs I encounter at the office and on crowded trains.* She envisions Maud clad in a tailored suit and seated behind a mahogany desk aptly managing an office.

Maud's sitting posture remains erect. Now she sits with folded arms dumping stares at Millie's suede pumps. Soon her hand dives into her crumpled shopping bag and fishes out a grimy, weathered pair of winter boots that are smaller than her feet.

Maud tries frantically to force the boots onto her massive feet. She pants, pulls, and even resorts to using the back of her hairbrush, but to no avail. The boots will not slide unto her feet. Hence, she whispers a swear, slaps the chair and keeps on her smudged red flats that seem to fit her well.

Millie can't offer Maud her boots though. Although she has many at home in her closet; her size seven feet are smaller than Maud's. Plus, what would she wear home? Although, she could buy an inexpensive pair of sandals. So, Millie wrestles with the fact that she is fickle and wastes money unnecessarily on clothes and fattening desserts. She could sell her unwanted belongings and give the money to people like Maud—or simply donate to homeless shelters. She thinks of the untouched new clothes in her closet still with price tags. *Why do I own more shoes and stuff than I need?*

The pastor makes remarkable progress with the communion service and reads from his massive brown bible.

"What chapter?" Maud suddenly stands, asking.

"Don't know," Millie replies.

Maud frowns at Millie and seems ready to argue but turns away.

"What's the chapter?" Millie asks the senior woman in the back pew.

"Matthew 26:17-30," the woman replies, tossing a condescending glare at Maud.

Maud finds the chapter, stands tall and reads it deafeningly, stunning the pastor and the congregation. Her firm, articulate voice fills the sanctuary.

The parishioners slumped against the wall to evade her, spread frowns on fat, skinny, white and black faces ready to ridicule her unwelcome disruption of the flow of service. Millie is impressed though since she does not expect a crazy woman to so aptly navigate the bible and read verses. Secretly, she applauds Maud's boisterousness, not wishing to experience her lunacy alone.

A team of deacons hastily serves the grape juice. Maud takes a glass, sips half of it and after brief cogitation concurs with procedure and places the glass with the balance of the juice in the bench holder. When the pastor announces, "Drink ye all of it," she switches her juice with Luke's. He then extends an aggrieved Irish hand to restrain Maud, but retracts it, licks his lips, and stares intently at her. He reddens. Veins in his neck expand briefly. Maud ignores his annoyance and drains his glass.

He throws somber looks at her juice and mumbles "Disgusting. Geebag!"

Millie's face twists with laughter even as her stomach growls. She wishes she had taken a glass she could drain. She does not empathize with Luke for Maud's behavior because Maud has become her pew pal and although she is batty, she means no harm. She feels remorseful for not partaking in communion and for not dedicating her undivided attention to the service, but Maud's lunacy engages her.

Perhaps, Maud once had a husband who resembled the pastor. *But the pastor did stare at Maud for a second and anything is possible in America*, Millie thinks. She likes Maud's raw assertiveness, and she doesn't look older than thirty. She wonders what triggered Maud's madness. Does she have a family that loves her?

Millie ponders the uncertainties of life. She is a youthful thirty-two, but insanity or death won't wait while she fluffs her hair or saves for a new car. She will complete her Bachelor's degree since she only has an Associates. She will unfreeze her eggs and try again to have a child and grow and bless her family. Her encounter with Maud tips things into perspective and floods Millie's thoughts with a silly verse her elders whispered while toiling over new babes.

> Tiny tots are poop machines, that humanize,
> And reward who raise and mobilize
> Stalwarts, to seed and breed familial troops;
> All honeyed allies of loyal deeds,
> None bitter bleats of grim defeats.

Millie eyes the clock above the rostrum that shows 12:50 pm then turns her face towards the pulpit and the climaxing service. She hopes to board the train on time for her speedy return home. She will devour her pasta meal then relax and phone chat with Georgie. The pastor directs everyone to pray in twos for the state of the nation and forgiveness for transgressions against others. Millie will not partner with Maud even if her conscience pricks her.

"Partners. Partners! I need a partner," Maud says, and looks at Luke, then at Millie, who looks at the cherubim carved into the ceiling hoping that Luke would be considerate and pray with Maud. Maud stands shaking her hands impatiently like a child pleading for a lollypop.

Millie peers at Luke through the corner of her eye.

He stands with his head bowed reverently. His lips move with inaudible prayer. "Rogue!" Millie mumbles. "He's no gentleman. Why does he subject me to her? Now I'm forced to hold her hands and feel her funk." Millie stands perplexed while Maud looks demandingly at her.

Murmurs of petitions fill the church from its diverse congregants.

Millie scrutinizes the church. A chunky Indian woman overcome by the Holy Spirit paces back and forth crying: "Thank you JE-EE-SUS. HAL-LE-LU-JAH." The woman looks possessed with disheveled hair and clad in a red and pink sari. Her eyes seem unfocused, but she's in bliss and oblivious to the stares stunned parishioners throw her way. Those standing still grasp tiny goblets and intentionally *ignore Maud. Maybe God condemns them and will deny heaps of starry crowns.*

Maud stamps her right foot indignantly. "Somebody better pray with me," she says, ringing her hands. Luke glares at her incredulously, and failing to recover from annoyance, grabs his elegant, grey jacket and leaves.

Millie groans as Luke's departing feet topple Maud's large, rumpled bag. The bag falls open. A jagged knife lands against Millie's right ankle. "Hee-el-elp" she screams. Her heart thumps anxiously within her chest. Over two hundred parishioners freeze with dumbfounded stares. Nobody comes to Millie's rescue. Nobody even records the scene with cellphones like true New Yorkers do.

Maud snatches her knife off the carpet and waves it menacingly with a feral glare. Then she tugs Millie's gorgeous Liz Claiborne bag. Millie shudders and yields the bag over. Maud examines its contents, ignoring Millie's cash and the clammy halve of her sandwich that she gifted Millie. She grabs instead, a russet lipstick from Millie's purse and dabs it expertly onto her demented lips. Maud then stoops and grabs a rusty mirror from her fallen shopping bag. She holds the mirror up pompously and slowly surveys her face.

"This lipstick is dull. Try crimson red," she says. She throws the purse back at Millie and continues to wave her knife, that is encrusted with rust, menacingly at those nearby.

To Millie, Maud has ballooned into a binging lunatic that enlarges each second. Her braids morph into horns that wave rebukes at Millie, the functional. Parishioners remain diminutive and too shocked to help.

Millie's stomach folds and feels queasy. She's not ready to die. Not even in a church. She loves attending plays and having philosophical chats with her husband. She loves apple picking in the summer and building snowmen in the winter. She cherishes the notion of having babies and raising a family with Georgie and playing with future grandkids. They will build a legacy and enjoy their children and retirement. And be "Stalwarts to seed and breed familial troops". Georgie will take her to his dear Guyana where they'll eat mangoes and dance to endless calypso.

The future flashes before her in seconds, summing up the value of life and the injustice of a stranger to nab it all. "He-ee-elp," she wails, as Maud leans over her and the strange day blurs then fades from view.

Millie's collapse lingers for a few miserable seconds before a pair of sturdy brown hands lift her to the respite room and a deep male voice asks, "Miss, Miss, are you okay?" Millie gulps her saliva and sits weakened with fear. She ignores the deacon before her and looks through a window screen, into the sanctuary at the clock that shows 12:57 pm.

Two deacons hustle Maud out of the church. She

kicks and yells about squalid scoundrels confiscating her constitutional rights, and that a church isn't a sanctuary if everybody isn't welcomed. And how dare they lay hands on her. "I'm the pastor's wife," she says. "You can't oust me from this church. I'll smash your skulls." She wrestles with the men and claws the face of a black deacon. He yells and takes his grip off of her shoulders. "She's a demon!" he says crossly. "Call the police, somebody."

Millie's teeth shake uncontrollably, forcing her lips to part like Israel's red sea. A deaconess fans her, and mops fear off of her face. The deaconess seems unfazed by Maud's outlandish brawl and is generous with chatter.

"I know she crazy, crazy," the deaconess says. "She always sitting and talking to herself, saying she's the pastor's wife." Millie flinches and gazes at the deaconess' creased face.

Flesh pleats around her waist and arms and she looks seventy-plus. Her hair is smeared with gray. Her brown eyes give a mischievous sparkle. Her voice sounds familiar. She is the prattling senior who sat behind Millie's pew.

"She sashays in here twice a month and takes a back seat. I reckon you was her friend. Ha, ha! You okay, Precious?"

"I'm fine," Millie says then scowls because her head aches. She misses Georgie and the sanctity of her home. She wants him to return from his native Guyana and comfort her.

She should have visited with him but had stayed her trip until summer 2008 in the new year when they'd celebrate their 4th wedding anniversary in his exquisite country that she has never visited. His Guyana must be divine because anywhere with him is a bliss. He's the kind of husband that folds you into him and you never want to lose his safe and clement embrace or miss the wisdom and salve of his words because he listens more than he speaks.

"You got a blessing," the old woman asks, and Millie jolts back into reality. "The Pastor give a good, good communion and I notice you didn't take none. You shouldn't dodge communions...."

Millie sits erect on the sofa pounded by this woman's blather. She can't fathom why she suddenly feels so tolerant towards this chatty deaconess after being traumatized. What blessings has she received? Perhaps her tolerance and endurance has improved. She longs to scream, "BE QUIET," but won't since this woman doesn't mean any harm and you must revere the old.

"Thanks for helping. I'll leave now," She tells the deaconess and rises.

"It's my duty, precious. Have some water first."

The old deaconess ambles off to get water and Millie grabs her purse and rushes out of Balm SDA Church. The clock chimes as she exits—one loud, protracted chime. *Had she really spent just one hour with God?* Service seemed eternal although so brief.

Millie tosses Maud's horrid sandwich into the garbage, then looks at the unbreakable afternoon sky and blinks at its brilliance.

Notes

Notes

TWO REMARKABLE NOVELETTES: VOLUME 1   Sheron Mingo Y

Turn Around Age

Things tumble into Ms. Meddlepearl's diary in August 1985: the eminent President Burnham dies, socialist Guyanese mourn, and Ms. Meddlepearl loses her housekeeping job and arrives at Prissy Senior Mansion in Georgetown, Guyana with her aged pain and a bucket of pride. The seniors recoil, and shun her because she's striking at sixty-eight and remains aloof, and says she's no "old fart." Eight-five-year-old Dewdroppy is smitten with her beauty and pursues her upon her arrival at Prissy. Months inch by and end the year with Ms. Meddlepearl grumbling and bullying and rejecting Dewdroppy's advances.

The new year delivers the first Wednesday afternoon of March, 1986 and Ms. Meddlepearl peers through her curtains, beyond her window, after she hears a familiar pant and rustle outside. She is barely able to suppress her giggles. The enamored Dewdroppy taps lightly at her bedroom door and places his unrecognizable self-portrait and a cube of guava cheese in a calabash beside her door.

"Gwan. Gwan, Dewdroppy. Don't you pester me," she whispers behind her closed bedroom door, so the other seniors won't hear and peep and create a spectacle.

"You can't reject me, Ms. Meddlepearl," he whispers

back. "My Mamma run way from me and Father when ah was nine. My wife died ten years now. Women keep running way. You must marry me and keep me."

"No, man! You too, too botheration and mannish," Ms. Meddlepearl replies, slapping her door so he'd vamoose as he eventually does. The dejected Dewdroppy leaves his coined poem behind with his calabash of gifts. She waits until he's gone to open her door as she deems it improper to encourage a man at her bedroom door, especially after 5 pm. Hence, she opens her door stealthily and snatches the calabash and reads his poem with a belly of giggles:

> Sweet lady dove, you are love.
> A daily taunt,
> My sugary want.
> Look at your smile: my toil for a wife.
> I'm waiting for you;
> We'll marry soon as you please.
> So, help me God,
>
> We'll marry soon as you please.
> You don't have to wash my clothes nor cook,
> But read romantic books.
> Nurse can fix while we eye the sunrise
> And waltz in the twilight's prize.
> It's old folks groove,
> When time moves.
>
> Cause we done all, bracing bumpy falls
> And life isn't fetching vigor

Nor loading favors.
Hurry and ditch the worry
So we settle and marry,
Cause, age isn't turning round,
Like no merry-go-round.

The night ends day. A fowl-cock crows next morning to announce the dawn of Thursday and a new Guyanese day. After breakfast, physical exercises, and an hour of deafening and mirthful singalong in Prissy's gym, the seniors freshen up and Dewdroppy follows Ms. Meddlepearl into the sprawling, grassy yard that skirts Prissy.

The blazing 10:30 am sun adds sheen to Dewdroppy's mirthful face. He sits erect although his skin lolls like crumpled satin upon his six-foot frame. He whistles proudly nonetheless and sports a gregarious smile. They sit at a little bamboo table on chairs that face the seawalls and Prissy's front gate to play *Snakes and Ladders*.

Ms. Meddlepearl knows it's March 6, Dewdroppy's birthday, and that he's too proud a Pisces to celebrate fearing she'd tease him about his age. She also knows from the other old folks that the date is significant to him because his mother had run away from him on a Thursday morning in March almost eighty years ago. *She'll be agreeable to honor his birthday,* she decides *and any gloom he may harbor.*

Dewdroppy inches his bamboo chair closer to Ms. Meddlepearl's as they play the board game, *Snakes and Ladders*. She ignores him and sips soursop drink from an enamel cup. She will evade his snakes and climb the ladder to victory if she rolls her die well, and moves her token along, and not get distracted like she usually does.

Perspiration washes Ms. Meddlepearl's smooth, chestnut toned temples: so, she rests her cup on the bamboo table beside their game and tucks her curly, silver mane into a bun upon her head. She reclaims her cup and continues sipping the fruity beverage that cools her tongue as she studies the menacing, coiled snakes threatening to forfeit her desired win. She pretends not to hear Dewdroppy in the adjacent chair passing a putrid wind.

Today young, young and fiery, unlike my old bones, she thinks. *Time does tire us like bed tire sheets.* She sits primly, straightening the yellow polka doted pleats on her frock with her thumb.

Two Indian men sit on piles of cut grass and drain coconut water from gigantic coconut shells, quenching their thirsts and filling their bellies. They arrive weekly to weed the yard with gleaming cutlasses. Their sweaty shirts are twisted into sodden knots around their waists to liberate their coffee arms and chests. Their legs gleam like cassava sticks dowsed in sweat.

The freshly cut grass beneath Ms. Meddlepearl's sandaled feet feels stubby like an unshaved chin. She sweeps the stubs with her sandals. A rich scent of fresh earth rises to her nose, and forces her to sneeze into her cotton handkerchief before her finger pushes the die up the ladder on the board game. Dabbing her nose, she stares briefly ahead at Prissy's closed gate. A munificent businessman built Prissy; he earned overseas profits exporting gold. "Let destitute seniors live their final years and expire gracefully," the man had said.

A white concrete fence surrounds the sturdy mansion that reaches three stories like an orange brick fortress with its 65 rooms. The mansion is crested by a pointy bell tower that tolerates 12 seniors at a time for quick oceanic peeps through an antiquated, but prized telescope. Dozens of palms, banana, soursop, cherry, and guava trees supply natural beverages and sweet treats for Prissy's old folks.

A thriving kitchen garden sprawls in the backyard, birthing stout breadfruits, thick leaf callalloo, green squashes and more to tender the seniors' daily victuals. The sea whirls and howls at high tide before the mansion like a caged vagabond. Stony seawalls strap it, restraining its salty waters from grabbing the old folks when they sit to enjoy the tropical breeze with sprays of the brackish sea wetting their faces.

Ms. Meddlepearl's eight months at Prissy dangle like eternity in her dreams; since her days and weeks don't seem to end, and old folks just sit around gauging hours.

Dewdroppy came ten years before in nineteen-seventy-five when socialism was thriving with the then President Burnham holding the reins and Guyana being self-reliant and flouncing hope. Meddlepearl knows that Guyanese Indians and blacks remain at odds; as it's alleged that the Indians eat pepper on rice, and own farms and cane fields: while many blacks flash showy government jobs and own teensy, weensy wealth.

Most Portuguese own furniture and merchandise stores and have marvelous homes. Chinese own restaurants and some of the few Guyanese whites remain aloof as international diplomats, in grandiose Brickdam houses, with autonomy to cross international borders.

Some Guyanese reject socialism and fret that the rich people in politics take bribes and hoard Guyana's wealth. Dewdroppy holds such notions. He was a shoemaker by trade and got tired of mending pompous government ministers' shoes for measly, hand-to-mouth earnings. Now he leans his lanky frame forward in his chair, overwhelmed by ardor, to stare into Ms. Meddlepearl's fascinating brown eyes, and almost knocks over his board die.

"Marry me. You'll vex heaven if you give your virtue to the cold indifferent earth. Look at them brown sugar legs of yours. Oh, my, my! The best ah seen."

He mumbles lines from his favorite poem coined especially for Ms. Meddlepearl.

> ... Hurry and ditch the worry
> So we settle and marry
> Cause age isn't turning round
> Like no merry-go-round.

Ms. Meddlepearl pushes her chair away from the besotted Dewdroppy, blushing. "Heaven know best, Dewdroppy. You eighty-five and I aren't even seventy. Don't see how you'll balance your cane and me."

"Ah will. Marry me and you'll see how independent Ah am.

Ah got twelve-hundred dollars stashed at the New Building Society Bank. We'll leave Guyana's socialism. Let the People's National Congress keep they stupide politics. Cause these two parties always warring and never bothering to serve the country. Let's you and me grab our freedom and go to North America and rent an apartment. TV and money plenty over there in the lands of dreams. Ah will find me a job and hire us a housekeeper. We'll start a nice little business and live like royalty and you'll be happier than Eve was in her garden."

"Dewdroppy, what you know about keeping a housekeeper? Thought you PPPs freed people. Least socialism keeps everybody roving merrily along with self-reliance and something to own. Overseas is the same with they robbing blacks and poor, poor people. You don't know North America capitalists fat on they greedy, spiteful capitalism? How we going to survive there in we black skins?"

"Just you marry me, Ms. Meddlepearl and forget 'bout your politics nonsense. Ah isn't no scholar."

Ms. Meddlepearl sucks her teeth long and hard. "Well, know the facts before you come condemning PNC people. We proud, proud comrades." A frown creases Ms. Meddlepearl's face. "We only want equality so everybody owns Guyana. Nothing wrong with planting and reaping our foods. Pretty soon we feed other countries and fetch they money so we growing burly, burly and nice. "Guyana's my home. That snowy North will freeze my bones and start my aged pain."

"But Ms. Meddlepearl, you don't like living at Prissy. And them housekeepers make they honest keep."

"You're a real, real nuisance!" Ms. Meddlepearl replies not wishing to lose the argument. "I said I aren't going to no freezing place. I'm staying here, in my Guyana, and sip my soursop drink. Do you understand that?" Dewdroppy sighs and wipes his forehead. His sulkiness gives him a boyish vigor that envelopes him with charm.

Ms. Meddlepearl doesn't care that Dewdroppy sulks. She resolves to speak her mind forgetting it's his birthday and she should be agreeable with a pieces and on his special day. She watches him lean over and pluck a pink hibiscus from a branch that garlands their chairs and wonders whether he'll suck the sweet juice from the flower like most Guyanese do.

"You take this hibiscus," he says and graciously tips his imaginary hat.

Ms. Meddlepearl sticks the flower into her dress pocket with the petals flapping over her bosom like a Parasol. She likes Dewdroppy, but she won't surrender easily. She decides that he must hear her story and know that she once earned her keep and was independent, so he doesn't think she's some hand-to-mouth. He has no business plotting to win her heart and then drag her out of Guyana.

Fried mackerel and boiled breadfruit please her stomach. The sun blazes, but a cooling breeze comes. She's got the aged pain from falling, but it's calm when her walking and sitting postures are relaxed. Her heart must be healthy since it pats inside her chest and her feet don't swell like other old folks. She'll make do with Prissy and curb her fiery tongue. But she will eye the interfering Elsa who dotes on Dewdroppy.

Oh the dreadful, dreadful Old Higue! Ms. Meddlepearl hisses each time she encounters the roly-poly, ninety-year-old Elsa.

Ms. Meddlepearl leans forward and smoothens her dress with her right palm, then crosses her stockings legs and sits primly in her chair. The pleats on her dress don't seem circumspect today. The aged pain in her back throbs, but she doesn't complain. Butterflies dance around her head and she eyes their twirls and vibrant yellows, blacks, whites and browns from her comfy chair. She also notices two grasshoppers flirt and intertwine. There's nothing else to do with life at Prissy, but play board games and lime about the yard to divert time.

Ms. Meddlpearl suddenly frowns then pushes the game away; she thinks of how she gets no family visits but Elsa does.

Her family has expired except for her seventy-year-old sister who hopped on BWIA in 1970 and landed in Ontario, Canada. She never answers Ms. Meddlepearl's phone calls nor responds to her letters. Ms. Meddlepearl deems this stuck-up and cruel, and after feeling disconsolate about losing her job and cherished Guyanese independence, she wrote telling her sister to keep Canada and their British rule and she'd keep her Independent Guyana.

"I'd rather be Third World and a happy, happy comrade," Ms. Meddlepearl turns and says to Dewdroppy. "I won't have no cult leader poison me. What would I want with Kool-Aid when I got our nice, nice sorrel and five-finger drinks? You must be crazy." She stares at a snake lurking at the bottom of a ladder on the board game and decides that America's Kool-Aid must have tasted better in Guyana. Why did the Jim Jones folks want to die in her Guyanese paradise?

Ms. Meddlepearl, rising from her chair, tosses sugarcane husks into the rubbish bin, and then pulls her chair away from Dewdroppy and his rotten flatulence. He thinks she doesn't hear or smell, but she eyes him curiously thinking, *what a silly bother!* The midday sky sprawls like an indigo sea. The sun blazes, eager to roast her chestnut skin. She abandons Dewdroppy and the Snakes and Ladders game. She walks aimlessly, dodging the sun's glare each time it changes, and stands under the shady coconut palms for some refreshing breeze.

Life could be worster, worster than dodging the morning sun, she decides.

Dewdroppy rises slowly, but resolutely from his chair. He follows her enjoying the breezes beneath the brilliant blue sky and the coconut palms.

At 12:00 pm when the sun is sharpest in the sky, Ms. Meddlepearl and Dewdroppy sit inside Prissy with other seniors at dainty dining tables. They chow down curry fowl and rice for lunch with pieces of crunchy fried breadfruit. Ms. Meddlepearl sucks marrow from a juicy fowl foot and licks her fingers and lips counting the twenty dining tables filled with noisy seniors.

The three women and one man at her table eat quietly and smile with Dewdroppy, but avoid direct, or prolonged contact with her not wanting her scolds and arguments.

Ms. Meddlepearl wipes her mouth primly with her handkerchief then rises from their table and returns with Dewdroppy outside. Both paddle fat bellies as they settle into bamboo chairs. They sit facing the ocean that seems distance away from Prissy, and happy for the shade of the coconut palms above their heads. Dewdroppy sits gleefully and lets loose a dozen belches and grabs her hand.

"Leggo my hand," she says, although she enjoys his attention. "Man, you really, really botheration." She elbows him gently but yields her left hand then with her right hand places her yellow polyethylene bag upon her knees and her yellow frock. Dewdroppy swats a cheeky mosquito that alights on his pants, but he holds her hand as if she'd bolt like a nanny-goat.

"I say, leggo my hand. You're a damn pest," she tugs her hand away. "You always passing wind and belching." He conceals his shock at her knowledge of his daily plethora of flatulence.

"Ah got to do what ah got to do," he replies, sulkily, sucking his lip. "Old people can't turn 'round what years fetch."

She makes fists with her palms so he can't pry them open.

"I was independent. I earned my keep," she says proudly. "I didn't want to come here. I come 'cause I got sacked from Mr. Emanuel's employment. And I had no place else to go live."

Ms. Meddlepearl sighs determined to tell her story. Elsa had called her a liar days after her arrival. She hasn't been genial with Elsa since, and deems her a bad-minded nuisance for doubting her without any knowledge of her employment with Mr. Emanuel. She's a spiteful-jealous Old Higue, that Elsa, Ms. Meddlepearl had decided and wrinkled her brows with determination to harbor a rancorous relationship thenceforward.

Dewdroppy presses a button on his cane that opens his umbrella over them to intercept the scalding sun that peers through a palm branch. Ms. Meddlepearl's cheek burns with a blush; she appreciates the sudden transformation of his walking cane into an umbrella.

She thanks him slyly, and rolls her stare over him. She ogles the mole on his nose that jumps with mirth and mischief when he laughs. His brown, rosy lips trap an amiable smile. His clothes smell fresh of starch and fit him well. *But he always sucks his fish bones noisily,* she thinks. *The other old goats whisper and laugh at him. Maybe she could culture him. Her daddy taught her to sit erect and chew with her mouth closed.*

Nah! Nah! She recants. *Dewdroppy's an old frog. He likes to eat and flirt. What a bother*! But she tilts her head to the right thinking intensely, internalizing a song she had memorized a few years ago:

> We age like mold
> Losing lofty goals,
> With time bolting
>
> Dumping age and change.
> Wish time could twirl like an endless chain
> Around the aging stick.
>
> I'd marry and cure my itch;
> Marry and cure my itch,
> Every wish and achy twitch.
> Perhaps own a car,
> A fancy, dandy place
> With kids to tend my cares.
> When I'm feeble and rusty with age.
>
> Wish I was twenty again
> With no inkling of pain.
>
> I'd marry and cure my itch.
> Marry and cure my itch,
> Every wish and earthly twitch.
> But who can fling time around,
> To wipe away fickle frowns?
> Best I tackle the jabs of age
> And brush the dusty years.
>
> Best I waddle with grace
> And front the face of fate.

At 1:30 pm Dewdroppy combs his head of soft, grey hairs and grins in his tin mirror. If he angles the mirror cleverly, he'll see Ms. Meddlepearl's lovely, chestnut-colored legs without her realizing his mannish scheme. This he does regularly making her think he's incredibly vain.

"Let us walk 'round the mansion and count hibiscus buds," he says.

"Okay. Don't mind moving my legs and seeing pretty, pretty flowers," Ms. Meddlepearl replies, and loosens her hair to free her bouncy curls knowing their afternoon walks usually take a lofty hour with her counting more of the new hibiscuses than the distracted Dewdroppy ever could. He plunges his tiny mirror into his pocket and scrambles to his feet: then he groans and presses heavily on his cane.

"Ma wit's younger than ma soul," he says, grinning. His starched khaki pants fill with a slight breeze. He walks tall even with a bent back.

Ms. Meddlepearl steps smart and prim and pauses occasionally to touch and count the new hibiscuses and has counted twenty-eight thus far on three trees. Her white sandals and stockings feet flaunt her cherry toenails that match her fingernail polish and lipstick. Her side curls bounce around her face; complements of Nurse Gracus who presses the old ladies' hair monthly with her hot iron comb and gives them each a fancy presence.

"How come you stayed single? Ms. Meddlepearl?"

Dewdroppy asks. He looks at her from head to toe.

"Thirty new red and pink buds so far," she says before responding. "Had no choice. The marriages I seen were shady with drunk, drunk men bullying and beating-up their wives."

"Ah counted five new flowers beside your counts," he replies.

"Then you pay attention and stop bothering me if you want to count plenty flowers," Ms. Meddlepearl says, noting Dewdroppy's naughty grin.

"Isn't life a taunt? Marriage is sweeter than swank when you love and cherish your mate. Close you brazen eyes and don' say a word."

"Don't know if I should, Dewdroppy."

"Close them and open your hands."

"You're asking plenty, plenty, Dewdroppy."

Ms. Meddlepearl closes her eyes hoping her heart survives her surprise. Her left finger tingles for the ring she expects. Shiny, yellow gold is the esteemed Guyanese gold that brides crave. She pictures a splendid, yellow ring that would gratify her old soul and mumbles, "yes," in anticipation of Dewdroppy's proposal.

There's movement in the grass and Dewdroppy places something cold and soft in her hands. The thing moves and she screams and jumps.

"What is it? What...you pestering old goat?" she asks

sucking her teeth in disgust, and flapping her hands.

"Ha! Ha! Ha!" Dewdroppy rubs his stomach and laughs. "You got all that mouth and you 'fraid of a itsy-bitsy frog. You're a coward, but a darling coward."

Ms. Meddlepearl walks away towards Prissy yelling "old fart-nincompoop." She doesn't want him to see her laugh, but she chuckles for being scared of a scrawny frog when there were worse torments in the world: like being fired from her housekeeping job and having to live at a senior's home when she doesn't feel tattered and impotent.

She pauses her walk not wanting to enter Prissy nor face Dewdroppy and leans against a robust cherry tree, on the freshly manicured lawn before Prissy's magnificent, wooden, front door. She stretches her right arm upwards and plucks a few rosy cherries from the tree to eat ignoring the juicy ones on the ground.

Sometimes the old folks are allowed to sit on the seawalls at low tide. They sit on chipped, concrete benches and complain saying they're being restrained like prisoners in a fortress with no family to visit them.

Once they come to Prissy, they lose their independence. Nurses say they're incompetent and they can't leave the yard without supervision. They're huddled and shuttled to church, the movies or the botanical gardens like donkeys and sheep. Or they sit at the seawalls and count the brown salty sands and the slaps of tossing waves.

Ms. Meddlepearl harbors thoughts of running away one day to reclaim her independence, but she won't board BWIA and fly to the chilly North. She'll rent a boat and row up the Demerara River where the warm sun nests and rainwater is fresh. She'll build a hut and live in the jungle like the Arawak Indians eating curried iguana and drinking creek water. Then she'll go and see the Kaieteur Falls and climb Mount Rorima to defy her aged pain.

Ms. Meddlepearl smiles with happiness sucking a juicy cherry with her back against the cherry tree. *Picture me with my bubbies hanging loose, loose like them Indians and a tiny cloth round my waist,* she thinks. *That is real, real wotless for womenfolk. But the Arawaks don't care none at all.* She laughs, intrigued, and looks at Prissy.

Perhaps Dewdroppy will come, but I won't have him chase me around all day for silly romance as if he was still a young man. She chuckles and tosses a cherry seed. Life would be perfect like when she worked for Mr. Emanuel and his children. *Now bad luck and age got her shackled as time slips away.* She sighs ruefully at the mansion—for it was indeed a safe place for old folks to live at.

Dewdroppy catches up with Ms. Meddlepearl and stands beside her under the cherry tree just as the church clock strikes 2:00 pm. His face anchors a contented smile.

His skinny legs move carefully within his starched khaki trousers over the grass—as if to test his steps. A lazy breeze puffs up his shirt-jack. He holds a grey kerchief ready to dab his brows.

"Come. Come. Listen," Ms. Meddlepearl says, tugging his arm. "I Kept house for Mr. Emanuel and his children after his cheating wife deserted him. I was independent before I came here eight months ago."

"How long you worked for him? Ah don't believe you. Ah sure ah seen you here more than eight months. Ah just hadn't the pluck to come woo you."

Ms. Meddlepearl ignores Dewdroppy's rotten wind. Old people can't control their winds, but some winds blow nastier than some. She exhales quickly, and then replies. "I worked for Mr. Emanuel, Dewdroppy. I failed as housekeeper. I'll tell you after I nap." They continue their leisure stroll around Prissy admiring the spread of pink, yellow and red hibiscus flowers. Walks help them digest their lunch. She sees Elsa spying from her bedroom window.

"That woman's really, really bad-minded!" she says, and sucks her teeth. "She'd drink my blood like a Old Higue if I let her, but the jealousy-goat don't frighten me. She want you and you want me. Let me see who get you!" Dewdroppy laughs with a wink but keeps his silence as Ms. Meddlepearl continues her venting. "She real, real stupide. If she want a man she should dress up nice, nice and comb her picky-

picky hair. She too, too wrong-sided."

Ms. Meddlepearl tosses her curls and faces the street looking at a dray-cart that rattles by with piles of plantains and plump, specked pumpkins until it disappears. The strapping horse drops steaming dung on the street and hurries like it's on some stately mission.

That galloping horse wears shackles like we old people, Ms. Meddlepearl thinks standing with her hands akimbo. She looks around the yard and at the mansion. *At least he can gallop some-where. Where I can gallop to? Eh, eh? Age and pain is a nuisance.*

A mongoose gnaws a rat and licks his mouth and paws near the foot of a Mango tree.

"That's nasty," Dewdroppy says.

Ms. Meddlepearl looks away from the street and says, "It's eating same as we. Let it be. Rats die so mongoose can stuff they face like we gobble up fowl foot and cow tongue."

"Don't get philosophical with me, Ms. Meddlepearl. We eating fowls and cows aren't nasty like a mongoose gobbling a rat."

"It is to the fowl and cow, Dewdroppy. They got souls like we."

"Bah! Ah was never good at logics. My mind's too fickle. Now tell me your story. Mr. Emanuel wouldn't fire a woman like you. He'd marry you if he was sensible. You all couldn't have children. Your womb and all, but he'd have a good wife though. He would." Dewdroppy looks her over and sighs. "Ah sure would like to kiss them lips of yours and hug you nice and good, for always." Ms. Meddlepearl frowns and turns away from Dewdroppy's probing eyes knowing full well he means to wed her and will have his day when she's good and ready.

"I spent twelve months and eight days with Mr. Emanuel and his children after my sewing job ended," she tells him. "You don't have to believe." Dewdroppy whistles and grabs her arm. Her heart races. "Lemego, you old-goat," she says defiantly. "Don't come hugging on me. Everybody will think we're a couple."

"Your bullying is a tease," he grins gallantly and says, then walks towards a garden bench. "Easy, easy, ah, here I plop my skeleton down. Pugh!"

The bench is hard, but his back is happy for the brace. He tilts his head and tickles his right ear. He belches long and hard then he scratches his back with his cane.

"Now go ahead with your story and don't digress! Old people must hurry with they business fore time mummifies them."

Ms. Meddlepearl chuckles about his antics and the silly names she christens him. "Okay, old gander," she says.

"Every morning at seven, Mr. Emanuel kissed the

sleeping children and drove away in his shiny, caramel Maurice car," Ms. Meddlepearl sitting happily by Dewdroppy, says.

"Oh! That's my favorite color. Did he really have a caramel, Maurice?"

"I said he did, Old Fart, didn't I? I don't lie," Ms. Meddlepearl says with a stern gaze.

Dewdroppy grins at her irritation. "Don't be grouchy. You too pretty for that. Go ahead and tell me that story. Ah will sit as still as the morning dew."

Nurse Princes meanders over and shushes a pesky beetle away. The tower clock announces 2:15 pm, in itssingsong voice, and Ms. Meddlepearl frowns because it's naptime.

"It's time for your afternoon siestas," Nurse Princess says.

"Shoo, shoo!" Ms. Meddlepearl replies, disgusted with the nurse's intrusion. "We old people knows what to do. We been around before you sprouted teeth."

"You must nap nonetheless," nurse Princes says.

Ms. Meddlepearl rolls her eyes and stamps her right foot. "I'm not moving nowhere."

"You must follow instructions, Ms. Meddlepearl. It's good for your health."

"That's all you young ones do, meddle and bully old folks 'round. Time somebody set you right. Here I'm sitting decently with this man and you pestering when nobody need any fusses."

"Come now, Ms. Meddlepearl."

"I'm telling him my story before I nap. You staying or you leaving?"

"Fine! I'll leave you two, but don't blame me for this fiery sun out here—it's way too hot, and old folks must wear hats and stay cool."

"Cluck, cluck." A rooster and hen flutter in fierce combat and the door to their coop swings open. Ms. Meddlepearl eyes the ruckus with disapproval since it interrupts the narration of her story. Orange, black, and brown feathers float to the ground. A mongoose sits in the bush eyeballing the dispute, hoping to devour one of the escaped fowls should any dart its way.

"Go on! Go on to hell, nuisance, Ms. Meddlepearl says wondering who left the coop open when it should remain closed. *Them fowls will fatten my guts.* "Catch them, Nurse before the mongoose does."

Nurse pitches a cane husk at the mongoose then shoos the liberated fowls over the paling towards their coop and runs after them. Two seem intent on flying over Prissy's brick wall. Nurse grabs one unruly fowl by its leg. The other flies towards the brick wall clucking resentfully.

"Hold this fowl," Nurse tells Dewdroppy. "And I'll go after the rooster getting away."

"Not me, nurse. Ah don't feel inclined to holdin' no ferociously cluckin' thing that will peck my fingers off."

Dewdroppy hobbles away and sneaks through Prissy's door and leaves nurse and Ms. Meddlepearl outside. Ms. Meddlepearl's face turns rancorous. She has lost her audience
and won't be able to finish her story.

"You hold this hen," Nurse says, shoving the feisty bird into Ms. Meddlepearl's hands before she could protest. Ms. Meddlepearl grabs the fowl like she did at Mr. Emanuel's if a fowl escaped his coop. But this fowl flies into the air and she falls clutching its legs and earns its peck and a run on one of her stocking legs.

"What a spiteful creature!" she says as Nurse dashes through the gate in pursuit of the rooster.

Ms. Meddlepearl's back stings and her old bottom tightens with pain. She rubs her back and glares at the squawking fowl in her grip. The fowl shudders and flutters its wings vigorously to protest her clutch on its yellow feet.

"I hope we gobble you up for dinner," Ms. Meddlepearl says and frees the fowl with a savage shove. "That'll teach you to cause a commotion and bump my aged bottom."

The horrified bird kicks, flaps its wings, and scurries into the coop.

Ms. Meddlepearl holds her back defying the aged pain that originated from her fall at Mr. Emanuel's house. She stares with a vexed scowl at the belligerent fowl now cowering in its coop. The throbbing in her back are tiny spasms at first that erupt into crescendos of discomfort. She turns on her side, but the pain turns with her refusing to ease.

"I going straight, straight to bed if I ever rise," she says, and crumples her face at a tiny spasm. "I hope this pain scram once I lay down. Nurse will have to give me tablets. I never have bad, bad pain like this."

She frowns at Prissy. *That old fart thinks I don't see him peeping from the door. He had better come help. That's what any decent man would do.*

Dewdroppy sticks his head out of Prissy's door then leans on his cane and waddles over to Ms. Meddlepearl. "Oh dear me," he says leaning on his cane and trying to pull her onto her feet but wobbles. "You must lose weight."

"Just be manly and lift me," Ms. Meddleppearl says, irritated with his insult and forgetting her pain. "One hundred-sixty pounds isn't heavy. I'm 5'6 tall."

Nurse Princes returns and springs to their rescue. She pulls the vexed Ms. Meddlepearl onto her feet and steadies Dewdroppy. But Ms. Meddlepearl's pride droops because her skirt hem leaps over her head and Dewdroppy enjoys a sly eyeful.

The sun glows in the sky and Ms. Meddelepearl needs her afternoon nap; what with falling and exposing her privates and all.

All three enter Prissy and go straight to the rooms. Nurse hugs Ms. Meddlepearl's arms and helps her into her fancy twin bed. It has pink, white and green floral beddings from Mr. Emanuel. She then gets a basin of warm water and a rag and gently saps the sore spot on Ms. Meddlepearl's back. Ms. Meddlepearl traces the flowers on her bedding, and sighs, thinking *how nice it is to have special gifts from Mr. Emanuel and wonders about him and his kids.*

"I'll get my rest now. You can go," she tells Nurse, after endless minutes, and lowers her back slowly to the bed. This feels better already.

"Get some sleep, then. You'll be perfect when you wake," Nurse replies.

Ms. Meddlepearl smiles placidly after the nurse leaves. Her back is a wreck, but not nearly as critical as she exaggerated for a nice back rub. She sighs sleepily, appreciating the special treat.

Ms. Meddlepearl sleeps contentedly and dreams that she's the queen of her home, with three young kids and a new baby, and Dewdroppy's her revered king. They own a two-story house up Guyana's Essequibo River. A chirpy buck woman sweeps and polishes their wooden floors weekly, and presses the lace curtains before hanging them. Fern plants and fresh air keep the house sweet and unfaultable. Ms. Meddlepearl takes their kids to the village school, weekly, on schooldays then nurses and plays with her baby. Dewdroppy makes dainty wooden tables and chairs, beds, and the baby's white crib. They mold exquisite clay plates and dishes, inscribe their initials and bake them in a hot-coal oven, in the yard, beneath the boundless sky.

In the evenings when the kids are fed and asleep, she slips into Dewdroppy's arms and watches the moon beguile the night. Then they out the lights and with renewed ardor celebrate their love as the stars spy through their bedroom windows from the heavens above.

The dream persists and dawn slips in and births a new day. Dewdroppy and their kids hurry to the creek to catch fresh trout and basha for their meals. Ms. Meddlepearl rakes the earth and plants balanjay, tomatoes, squashes, okras, pumpkins, and calloo. Her and the kids' arms shine with yellow gold and diamond jewelry. The baby and the 3-year-old girl are winsome with dimpled smiles and resemble Dewdrop. The 7-year-old and 5-year-old boys are rambunctious and as compelling as Ms. Meddlepearl. Hence she smiles, loving her enchanted dream.

At thirty-one, Dewdroppy toils in Guyana's thriving goldmines. He works zealously, for endless hours, seven months a year and returns with raw gold to sell and money to upkeep them for months. She beams serenely at the cooing baby girl in her arms and touches her breasts that are rich with milk. A burly black woman braids her hair weekly and makes fresh cassava breads for breakfast and cassareep they pour on meats. An old, avuncular Indian man cares for their brawny donkey and cow and gives the kids jolly rides and rodeos on the animals.

This is the free Guyana Ms. Meddlepearl adores were socialism lets everybody own and reap as much as they need and sow. Hence, she dreams on.

But reality soon dominates and a cock crows from Prissy's yard, announcing 4:45 pm, rousing Ms. Meddlepearl from her blissful dream. She stumbles out of bed, then promptly sits and rubs her back. "It's better," she says. "Just a little hurting now."

She lowers herself slowly to the floor with a wink and a smile, gets on her knees, and pulls her mostly empty green trunk from beneath her bed. The hinges make an eer-ee-ee squeak as she opens it and peeps in. She takes out the soft, flowing, terylene white dress with a delicate cascade of ivory lace on its bodice that her scandalous mama left before she ditched Ms. Meddlepearl and her sister and their father to run off with a stevedore.

She unfolds a yellowed, wrinkled note from her mama that reads, "Be worthier than me."

Tears fill Ms. Meddlepearl's eyes. She misses her evasive and defiant sister who will never be her maid-of-honor and know her joy when she marries Dewdroppy. *It wasn't nice not having a mamma and now a sister to talk to and ask women-stuff.* "The nerves of them wretches," she says, then inches into the dress and forces the zipper up.

"I hope this dress brings a river of luck. I really, really shouldn't dress-up in it before my wedding day. I'll have to pray mamma's blight away."

Ms. Meddlepearl pats her belly and forces her saggy tit-tits up with her arms. "I have to lose some weight to keep my health, but I'll be a comely bride and a good wife if I ever marry Dewdroppy. I'll brew his tea and soothe his sore leg. Ha, Ha! Picture me taking a husband when I thought I'd remain an old maid." She kisses her dress, returns it to the trunk, and pushes the trunk beneath the bed. The paper stuffed between her bosoms pokes her skin. She yanks it out, unfolds it, and reads Dewdroppy's poem.

> Sweet lady dove, you are love.
> A daily taunt,
> My sugary want.
> Look at your smile, my toil for a wife,
> I'm waiting for you.
> We'll marry soon as you please.
> So help me God,
> We'll marry soon as you please.
> You don't have to wash my clothes nor cook,
> But read romantic books.
> Nurse can fix while we eye the sunrise
> And waltz in the twilight's prize.

It's old folks' groove,
When time moves.

Ms. Meddlepearl reads Dewdroppy's poem repeatedly before refolding it carefully and tucking it back between her bosoms. Then she gets into her ironed afternoon dress with the green stripes and thick white sash. The tiny rip on her stockings will stay. She therefore refreshes her powder and lipstick and marches to the front room with a sigh for the aged pain that's awake in her back. Dewdroppy plays dominoes and flirts with Elsa and Pansy. Ms. Meddlepearl pouts and stamps towards them.

"Dewdroppy, don't talk to her. She's a hand-to-mouth- jealous-old hag. Come along and I'll finish my story."

"You's a spiteful-ignoramus and nothing good...!" Elsa says. "He been my friend ten years now. You just got here and you bully and hoarding him. Is what wrong with you?"

"He isn't your friend, Elsa. You meddlesome, nuisance! Don't pester him or I'll hide your album and you won't be able to parade those dreadful, stupide pictures of your relatives."

Elsa brandishes frustrated fists and glares at Ms. Meddlepearl, but doesn't move because she's half Ms. Meddlepearl's size. "You's a cantankerous jombie," she says instead with her head down. "You come to Prissy with you fancy, dandy talk and months of trouble. Dewdroppy doesn't love me no more and it's all your fault." Tears tumble from Elsa's eyes and she blows a snotty nose.

"That woman is a brawling nuisance!" Ms. Meddlepearl points distastefully at Elsa. "Come along," she pulls Dewdroppy away from the table and smiles triumphantly. He frowns and leaves Elsa. "Ah hope your back's better." He says. "That fiery tongue of yours don't show no pain."

"It's better, thank you," Ms. Meddlepearl replies, smiling gracefully as they glide away. They sit in corner chairs on Prissy's veranda with lovely views of the sea and gentle whirs of the evening breeze that tickle their ears and cheeks. A Brazil nut tree rises above the roof and flings brown leaves and dead buds to the ground.

The endless sea swells for miles and enchants their eyes as countless sails flutter in the distance, to drift their foreign ways. Ms. Meddlepearl wonders where the ships are headed with their salt-fish, bananas and other Guyanese produce, taking the best and leaving them the pittance. *North Americans must relish tropical victuals. We got real, real food and they got the money.* She decides that perhaps trading is fair since everybody should gain something—so she sings.

> Sail away, sail away rushing fleets,
> With produce to trade
> And money to rake.

Let the world see
Guyana earns her keep;
Sugar and rice,
Bauxite, timber and spice.
Pile the eminent yellow gold,

Sail away, sail away as you're told
Beyond brown salty deeps;
Cross the equator into chilly seas,

Sail away, sail away jolly old fleets.

A BWIA plane floats by, with its massive white fuselage and blue strips, transporting hundreds. Ms. Meddlepearl notes this with a sigh and decides those on flight are foolish to leave Guyana for the frosty North. A jombie bird perches on a coconut tree in front of Prissy. Ms. Meddlepearl waves her arms at it frantically, alarmed at potential calamity since everybody knows that jombie birds don't gather their wings and leave alone.

"Scram! Scram, jombie-bird. You're a nuisance," she says. "Take your calamitous omen. Scram, scam. Nobody must die." She makes the sign of the cross on her heart turning her back on the unwelcomed bird and her fervent rival Elsa and facing her loyal Dewdroppy. He scratches his head and smiles at her. "That sunset is a crimson kiss," he says, and winks.

"Means passion for the night. That's how life will be once we married. Now finish your story."

Ms. Meddlepearl tells how she had given the

children scrumptious bakes, fried crunchy in oil with saltfish choka and sweet broom tea, each afternoon, and how the little boy ate and laughed and made a mess she gladly cleaned.

"Oh gees! Ms. Meddlepearl, ma stomach's grumbling. We must ask nurse for a taste of supper. Yes, that's what we will do."

"You're a terrible, terrible bother," Ms. Meddlepearl says standing over Dewdroppy with hands on both her hips and squinting her eyes. "We could never be husband and wife. You always hungry and you aren't doing nothing, but sitting. Can't you listen for a minute?"

"Your minute is perpetuity. Ah going to Prissy's kitchen to get sweet broom tea and salt biscuits from the cooks."

Dewdroppy rises and disappears into Prissy for a while then returns with a wobbly swagger, balancing a tray and wearing a winning smile. Four of his front teeth are missing, but his slender cheeks are shaved and smooth. His slim mustache jerks up and down as he smiles.

"Here, Ms. Meddlepearl, have some sweet broom tea and pickled mango. Elsa made pickled mango."

"That obeah woman! I won't have her evil pickled mango. She's bad, bad news. I don't want her blight. I told you not to keep her company."

"Don't row. Ah won't speak to her no more."

"I can have your tea if you listen to my story. Pitch Elsa's nasty pickle in that bush or you going to dry-up and wither like paddy husk."

"But ah want the mango and the pickle look nice and thick."

"Toss it or I won't ever, ever speak to you." Ms. Meddlepearl stamps her right foot for emphasis.

"Okay. Okay lady," Dewdroppy says then wipes his hand and stares at the dusky, blue sky. "Now, finish your story," he says. He sips his tea, still looking dolefully at the pickled mango.

"I will, if you listen. Three-year-old Daniel bite me once. What a calamity! My arm got the scar. I'll show you once I finish this story," Ms. Meddlepearl says and winks.

Dewdroppy presses closer to her and she doesn't object. She wants him to listen. Plus the depraved Elsa has followed them with her barefaced ogling. Ms. Meddlepearl rolls her eyes at Elsa, then makes a defiant face showing her tongue. Dewdroppy is clueless of their prolonged combat since they moved to the veranda, but she slyly fights Elsa with her eyes unbeknownst to him. He fishes out his handkerchief and mops his brows then combs his hair and looks at Ms. Meddlepearl's legs through his tin mirror. He listens for a while to her story and then submits to sleep and amorous dreams of her wrapped securely in his arms.

The evening clouds likewise paint imaginary lakes,

hilltops and myriads of ambiguous fancies that will soon slip behind the night when the sky turns imperial blue. Prissy will serve dinner in 45 minutes, at the pinnacle of 6:30 pm, to dozens of eager and noisy seniors seated at tables. Ms. Meddlepearl's nose conjures up the arresting sweet, burnt smell of sugarcane bubbling in a factory and she's unsure of whether the smell is real or surreal since the factory is miles away up the East Bank.

Blue jays and chickadees fly by with sweet evening whistles. A brown grasshopper jumps on Dewdroppy's head and hops onto his ears and rouses his sleep. He springs from his chair. Ms. Meddlepearl tilts her head and laughs until her sides ache.

"Tell your story," a mortified Dewdroppy says, as if nothing has happened but feeling hurts in his pride and his left leg. "Ah like the sound of your voice. Ah'd love to hear it always. Sounds like my Mamma used to, 'fore she run way with that fishmonger."

Ms. Meddlepearl looks at Dewdroppy. *He's a lunatic,* she thinks, *but he's a good man to keep. He's tired is all. But he shouldn't compare me to his mamma. I aren't no old fart.* She looks curiously at him then slaps his chair. "I'm not your Mamma. I'm Ms. Meddlepearl so keep your eyes open! I'll soon finish my story. Then we can have evening dinner with the old folks."

"Then your scar?"

"Then my scar," She replies. She continues her story with renewed vigor, determined to complete it before dinner, even if Dewdroppy sleeps. All she needs is his presence anyway. Sleeping people are usually half-awake. He wouldn't miss all of her telling of her mishap. She fishes a cherry lollypop from her bag and gives it a long lick that reddens her tongue. Ms. Meddlepearl speaks on, swinging her stocking legs to and fro beneath her chair.

"One day I decided to dress the children and take them for a walk before their father returned," Ms. Meddlepearl says and swats a fly off of Dewdroppy's head.

"The clock showed 3:30 and Mr. Emmanuel would be home at 5:30 pm. The girl, Pith, protested, saying she didn't want a bath. She wanted to sleep and dream of heaven where God and his angels lived. 'Come, come, Sweetheart,' I said. I usually won five-year-old Pith over with candies and hugs, but it didn't work at all that wretched, wretched day.

'Ms. Pearl, I don't want to bathe, and I won't,' the child had said, obstinately, dropping the first two syllables of my name as she usually did.

'You got to bathe, Pith,' I had insisted.

'You're not my mother. You can't make me,' Pith had replied."

Ms. Meddlepearl brushes a leaf off of Dewdroppy's head then licks her cherry lollypop before she continues speaking.

"I had stood tongue-tied. I didn't want Mr. Emanuel returning and finding his kids unkempt. I thought the situation a bad, bad calamity and lifted Pith to put her into the bathroom. The child screamed and kicked, and we struggled. I slipped and hurt my back and little Daniel who was seated quietly by the sink listening got whacked in his face. His lip swelled big, big, like a cherry and began to bleed. It was a real bad, bad situation."

"Hmm-mmm-mm," Dewdroppy says. His eyes are closed and intoxicated with sleep.

Ms. Meddlepearl shifts in her chair, glares at him and then continues her story.

"'See what you've done?' Pith had screamed. 'I'll tell my daddy when he gets home.' I grabbed Daniel and rocked him gently. He hollered like bolts of thunder and blood spurted from his lip. My body felt heavy, and my back ached terribly, terribly starting my aged pain.

I couldn't rise from the floor. I realized right there and then that I was useless. 'What a calamity,' I kept saying. 'You done me in, Satan.' I tried to wipe the blood from Daniel's mouth, but Pith kicked and clawed like a drowning kitten and wouldn't allow me. I sat there in that kitchen helpless and ravaged on the floor surrendering to a four-year-old bully." Ms. Meddlepearl sighs sadly but speaks on even as Dewdroppy enjoys his sleep.

"*Children couldn't give backchat in my days. They'd*

be flogged with a wild cane on they behinds, I had thought, and wiped tears from my dispirited face and realized that at sixty-eight I was older than I wanted to be. When Mr. Emanuel's car pulled into the yard, I willed myself slowly up and leaned against the sink anticipating his scolding.

Luck is a nasty, nasty old fart and a nuisance, I decided. Here I was enjoying my new family and home. Now I had nothing, nothing." Ms. Meddlepearl pauses for a moment and holds her heart before she resumes relaying her story to the sleepyhead Dewdroppy.

"'What's the matter? Good Heavens! Why is Daniel hurt?' Mr. Emanuel had grabbed Daniel and rushed to the sink. 'Call Doctor Smart, Ms. Meddlepearl. Daniel's mouth has a big gash. I thought I could depend on you to care for the little ones.'

'I'm sorry, Sir,' I had said.

'I don't want the children or you to suffer anymore injuries. I'll pay your salary until I replace you,' he replied.

I had gone to bed with a million tears, not caring if they heard my sobs. I liked living with the Emanuels and belonging. I counted him, my son and his children, my grands. Now I have no one. No one. The children needed someone younger who could romp and tend to their growing needs. I couldn't blame Mr. Emanuel for dismissing me from the dear job after just twelve itsy-bitsy months and eight days."

Dewdroppy sneezes then resettles in his chair. Ms. Meddlepearl jumps, startled, and glares at him.

"Ah listening," he suddenly says before he slips back into his enraptured sleep with a mirthful smile on his face.

She slaps the table; then she shakes her head reproachfully at him and continues her story.

"What a wicked, wicked mishap, I had said that day we hauled my suitcase thought these doors. Mr. Emanuel brought me here with a tear in his eye and wished me much luck. He said I should be happy at Prissy and make many friends. He'd send me gifts on my birthday and at Christmas. He was the one who got my room here at Prissy. Now after eight months my tears are still fresh, fresh."

Ms. Meddlepearl dries her eyes, hurriedly with her handkerchief. Dewdroppy snores like a Billy Goat and passes wind. He neither hears nor sees Ms. Meddlepearl's sobs. It would be a mortification to have him see her cry since she's prim and proud. *I'll marry Dewdroppy and stay at Prissy,* she decides. *I won't fret anymore. I'll try hard, hard to get along with the old people. Guess I can tell Dewdroppy my story when we marry. Cause he sit here fast asleep not minding me at all.* She takes the creased paper out of her bosom and reads his poem.

. . . Cause we done all, bracing bumpy falls,

And life isn't fetching vigor
Nor loading favors.

The 6:15 sky darkens as if to hide a frolicsome day. Ms. Meddlepearl kisses the paper, refolds it, and tucks it between her bosoms.

"Wake up, Dewdroppy," she says. "Open your botheration eyes. We'll get married and I'll show you my scar." She taps Dewdroppy's shoulder. He doesn't budge, but she smells his rotten wind. Her hand keeps tapping.

"Oh dear, the man won't wake, and his chest isn't heaving and falling like the living is supposed to. Don't play tricks on me. I'm sorry I bullied you. Wake up. Wake up, old fart. It's time for Prissy's dinner and you never miss dinners."

Ms. Meddlepearl looks, then pokes Dewdroppy. She even puts her finger beneath his nose to test his breading. She wrings her hands and walks in circles unsure of what to do. She couldn't live without a friend to love her. She's had no one to love her for most of her life and she won't let Dewdroppy leave her. "Nurse! Nurse, come here quick, quick. He won't wake at all."

"What happened?" Nurse Princes asks feeling Dewdroppy's pulse and fanning his face with a purple rag. She slaps his cheeks and ears and sees that he is playing tricks. Ms. Meddlepearl stands apprehensively and disapproves of the rough treatment of her love but is too afraid of his demise to object.

Nurse Princes shakes her head sympathetically with a sly smile. "It's a shame. Dewdroppy was a sweetheart," she says and suppresses her laughter.

"I tried to tell him my story, but he fell asleep. Now he won't stir," Ms. Meddlepearl replies with tears streaming from her eyes and wondering why Nurse Princes is not panicked nor more sympathetic.

"That was some story. I'm afraid he may never stir again," Nurse Princes says.

Ms. Meddlepearl remembers the blackbird that had circled earlier and wrings her hands and shudders. "But I must, must show him my scar. Who will marry me now?" Ms. Meddlepearl looks at her left hand and then dabs at her tears.

"I should have been patient with him," she says. "Oh, how could I be so, so mean to my old fart?" Ms. Meddlepearl hugs Dewdroppy's neck and kisses his cheeks like he's her lost goat. She can't lose everybody she ever has, her family, now her groom.

Dewdroppy suddenly sits upright in his chair with a brazen grin. "You can show me that dainty scar of yours whether ah dead or alive."

Ms. Meddlepearl screams in shock and happiness and holds her heart like she's afraid it'll fall to the ground and roll away. "I thought you had dropped dead, dead like the tomcat," she says.

"Ah breathing same as you. Ah had to scare reason into your lovely, sassy head."

Nurse stands with her mouth stuffed with laughter. She looks at Ms. Meddlepearl. She looks at Dewdroppy enjoying how he finally captured his beloved, spirited bride.

Ms. Meddlepearl's heart dances with elation for the sweet old fart that woos her. She holds his hands, not minding the wrinkles that grab her palms. "Tomorrow nurse can take us to the magistrate for a license," she says with a euphoric smile. "We'll have a wedding during dinner in the dining hall and invite all the old folks so everybody can eat and drink they full. I'll invite Mr. Emanuel and the children. And Elsa too. Everyone, everyone I'll invite. The reverend must bless our marriage. Then you can hear my story and see my scar."

"Ah much obliged, Ms. Meddlepearl," Dewdroppy says excitedly.

She frowns helplessly as his flatulence fills her nose.

"We'll move your things into my room soons as we marry," he says holding his ecstatic head and shoulders high and erect.

"A man must keep his bride by his side."

Notes

Notes

Enjoy Books By
Sheron Mingo Y

Current Books

Non-Fiction Cookbooks
Vegan Delectable: Volumes I-V

Literary Fiction
Two Remarkable Novelettes: Volume 1

Upcoming Books

Poetry Collection

Fiction
Two Remarkable Novelettes: Volume 11
& More

About The Author

Sheron Mingo Y is a Multi-Genre Writer, Author of *Two* "Remarkable Novelettes: Volume 1" and "Vegan Delectable: Volumes I-V Cookbooks. In 2003, she received the Roger B. Dooley Award for Creative Writing and a Frances Perkins Scholarship. Sheron received a 2007 Presidential award for literary volunteer work and won prizes at poetry and children's story open mic competitions.

Sheron is a Book and Publishing Coach and an entrepreneur, recognized as an *Alignable Local Business*

Person 2021 to present for Arverne NY.

Sheron lives in New York. She enjoys traveling and has lived and studied in Pennsylvania, Massachusetts, Germany and Costa Rica. She has a Bachelor of Arts degree in English, a Master of Fine Arts degree in Creative Writing and is a trained book publisher. Her writing is witty and authentic and presents the ugly and beautiful facets of life based on experience, observation and research.

Sheron values and respects others and expects decency from all people. She has experienced the ugliness and loveliness of life and considers herself a beautiful work in progress. Choose a topic and she probably has encountered it which enriches her writing and professional perspectives. She is passionate about motivating and sharing life experiences with others in the hopes of transforming and empowering others and helping to make the world a nicer place.

Sheron has been a vegan for 20 plus years and enjoys chatting with people, writing, coaching, creating gifts, cooking, hiking, jogging and traveling. Her life is governed and shielded by God, and she lives a devout Christian and will never deviate.

Sheron is a fount of literary creativity. Stay tuned for her poetry and upcoming books including her captivating novels. Check out Sheron's current books on amazon, her coaching at SheronMingoY.com and her brand items at *SuperMementosYea* online giftshop. Follow her on LinkedIn, X and Instagram and expect awesome experiences when you connect with Sheron Mingo Y.

Thanks for reading this Volume. Please leave a 5* review on any amazing aspect of this book.